Storm Codes

by Tracy Nelson Maurer

Illustrated by Christina Rodriguez

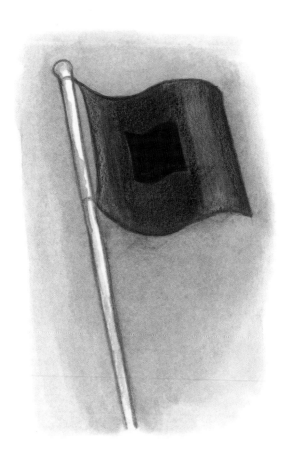

For Raquel,
Tooost! Toot-toot!
Tracy Nelson Maurer
3-7-18

Windward Publishing
AN IMPRINT OF FINNEY COMPANY

Storm Codes

Copyright © 2007 Tracy Nelson Maurer

Illustrations copyright © 2007 Christina Rodriguez

ISBN 10: 0-89317-063-1 hardcover
ISBN 13: 978-0-89317-063-9
ISBN 10: 0-89317-064-X softcover
ISBN 13: 978-0-89317-064-6

All rights reserved. No part of this book covered by the copyrights herein may be reproduced or copied in any form or by any means—graphic, electronic, or mechanical, including photocopying, taping, or information storage and retrieval systems—without written permission of the publisher.

10 9 8 7 6 5 4 3 2 1

Printed in the United States of America

Windward Publishing
AN IMPRINT OF FINNEY COMPANY

8075 215th Street West
Lakeville, Minnesota 55044-9146
www.finneyco.com

In memory of Captain Harvey Almstedt and his First Mate, Alice Almstedt –TMNM
For Barb and Steve Wood –CER

November's roaring northeast wind drove snarls of rain against our kitchen window. **_Fwap! Fwap-fwap!_** Heavy raindrops froze and stuck to the glass. They piled on top of each other and grew into a thick curtain of ice. I could not see the harbor lights down the hill from our house anymore. I hoped my father could see them from his ship on Lake Superior.

"How far out is Papa's boat?" I asked Ma. Her knitting needles paused and she shrugged her shoulders.

"I don't know, Katy," she said. "They should have docked hours ago." She glanced at the ice-smothered window across from her place at the kitchen table and scowled at the hazy view. Then Ma smiled at me and the knitting needles started to click again. "I'm sure Papa is fine."

Papa's empty chair at the table seemed ready for him to come home tonight. I was ready, too.

Papa was a captain on a Great Lakes steamship. He crisscrossed the Great Lakes from early spring to late autumn. During the shipping season, he stayed a night or two at our house between his trips. Mostly, we visited him when he unloaded and picked up cargo in Duluth, Minnesota or Superior, Wisconsin. Sometimes we drove to a nearby port to see him, maybe to Two Harbors or Silver Bay. The shipping season usually ended by December and then he stayed home for the whole winter in Duluth.

I pictured Papa standing in his towering pilothouse giving orders to his crew. His ship, the *Edward B. Greene*, stretched some 600 feet long. Huge cargo hatches opened to the storage area below. Papa's ship often carried taconite—gumball-sized pellets of baked iron ore—from our port at the tip of Lake Superior to ports on other Great Lakes.

The taconite came from the Iron Range mines north of Duluth. The pellets fed the great steel mills in places like Chicago, Detroit, and Cleveland. Factories shaped the fresh steel into cars, refrigerators, and other useful things.

Last year, Papa gave me three taconite pellets for show-and-tell at school. Everyone liked looking at them. I called them my good-luck pellets. I tucked them in my jewelry box on top of my bedroom dresser. Ma said they were just balls of dirt.

Suddenly, a loud crack and a heavy thump just outside the dark window snapped my daydream.

"Oh, no!" Ma exclaimed, squinting to see through the icy window. Then she shook her head sadly and said, "The heavy ice knocked down your climbing tree." Now I really wanted to cry.

"Well, there's nothing to do about that old tree right now," Ma said before I could stop a teardrop. "Let's batten down the hatches, Katy."

I knew what she meant. Sailors said that when they made the ship safe during a storm. I wondered if Papa had battened down his hatches, too.

12

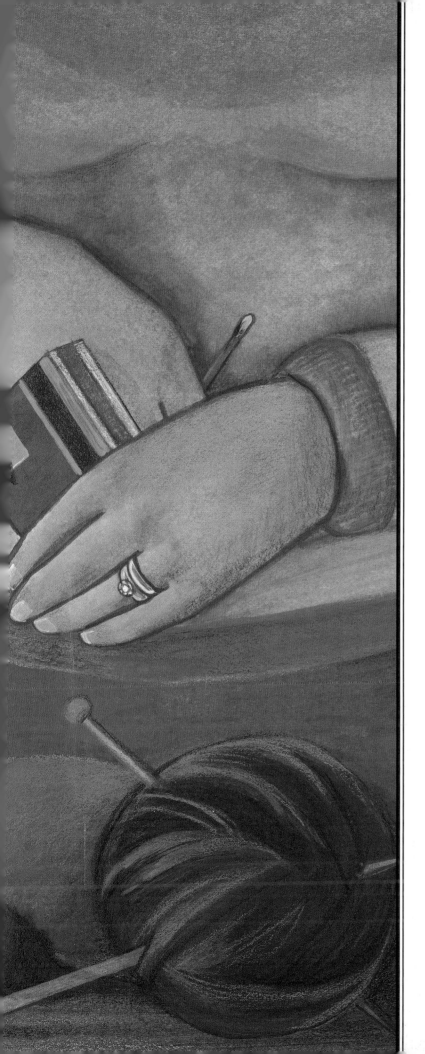

Ma set our old hurricane oil lamp on the table. I found the matches. She lit the lamp just in time.

The electricity flickered. The lights dimmed, then brightened again. A gust of wind rattled the windows and the room went black except for the hurricane lamp.

Ma settled back in her chair with her knitting. "Listen, Katy," she whispered.

At first, I heard only the wild rain and wind. Another tree branch cracked somewhere farther away. Then beneath the storm's tantrum, the sound came to me: *Baaaah-rum!*

The foghorn bellowed again. *Baaaah-rum!*

It kept time with the harbor's lighthouse that we usually could see from our kitchen window. The bright light flashed all night long, every night during the shipping season.

The sound and the light spoke to the sailors in codes. Each lighthouse along the Great Lakes flashed its giant beam differently than the others—two flashes every four seconds at one place, one flash every six seconds another. The codes helped the sailors find their way to the harbor, even in a fierce storm like this.

I imagined that my heartbeat was sending a code to Papa like the foghorn.

Buh-bump! Buh-bump! Buh-bump!

That meant, "Come home! Come home! Come home!" I sent my coded messages again and again and again.

I fell asleep sending my secret code. Ma must have put me in my bed. When I woke up, the morning sun was already melting the ice off my bedroom windows. I peeked through a clear patch on the glass. Everywhere trees bent to the ground under the heavy glaze. A gust of wind suddenly shook ice chunks off the trees. Silvery flashes filled the air, twinkling in the sunlight before they spun down to the cold ground.

Ma's coffee pot clanged on the gas stove and I smelled oatmeal cooking. I walked quietly into the kitchen, hoping Papa was sitting with her.

He wasn't.

"Mornin', Katy. Would you like some breakfast?" she asked.

"I'm not very hungry, Ma. Thank you, anyway."

"You need a hearty breakfast, my girl. We're going to the canal today and it's raw out there. Don't let that sunshine fool you," Ma said, already heaping the oatmeal into my bowl. Smothered under butter and brown sugar, the steaming globs almost tasted good.

"Are we going down to the canal to watch for Papa? Really?"

19

"The phone lines are down and the power is still out," Ma said as she settled into her chair at the table. "No sense in driving, since the ice is everywhere. So, we'll walk to the canal. If that's all right with you, of course." Ma smiled, knowing my answer.

I finished the oatmeal and we bundled up in our warm winter clothes. I pulled on my boots. Then I found the red hat and mittens Ma knitted for me last year. She wrapped the matching scarf around my face.

"Oh, wait, please. I forgot something," I said.

I clunked in my boots down the hall to my room and found my three good-luck pellets. I put them in my coat pocket.

I clunked back to the front door. Ma turned the knob and pulled. Nothing budged.

"Ice," she declared under her scarf. Then she gave the door a hard shove with her shoulder. She yanked the knob again. The door hinges crackled as they broke free from the ice.

We stepped outside. An invisible wall of wind slammed into us. Both of us quickly grabbed the metal railings on the steps to steady our feet on the icy stairs.

When we reached level ground, Ma asked, "What did you need from your room?"

"A little something for good luck," I said.

"Katy, you'll clean that coat yourself, if you put those dusty iron pellets in your pocket!" she scolded. I saw that a strand of reddish hair had unfurled from beneath her hat. Somehow it always did that whenever she felt angry or worried. The hair hung down on her forehead like the red warning flag that sailors used. Their red flag meant a storm was coming. Hers often meant the same thing.

I said nothing.

25

We picked our way along the icy sidewalk and down the hill toward the water. Mighty gusts whipped the waves in the canal. Frothy whitecaps peaked above the canal's breakwall. Sometimes the waves leaped over and spilled onto the sidewalk.

"Stay away from the water, Katy. Those breakers mean business," Ma said. "Let's sit on the bench over there."

Ma took out her binoculars and scanned the horizon. I could not see anything but the pounding waves and cold sky. A few seagulls fought against the wind. Most of the flock huddled on the rocky shoreline. I tucked my nose into my scarf.

The foghorn bellowed very loudly at the canal. All night it had called to sailors. I remembered my coded message and started sending it again to Papa.

Buh-bump! Buh-bump! Buh-bump!
"Come home! Come home! Come home!" I whispered to myself.

Ma said, "Ah, look! I see a boat!"

At this time of year, a lot of ships were making their last trips of the season before ice sealed the harbor. Maybe it wasn't Papa's boat.

I squinted. A dot appeared, then disappeared in the swells.

"Is it Papa's?" I asked.

"I can't see the color yet," she said. The grandly curved pilothouse on the *Edward B. Greene* sported an unusual shade of green. Ma knew many of the ships by their color, hull shape, or smokestack emblems. Papa's crew teased her that she was a better sailor than they were. She might have been. Ma helped Papa study for all the tests at the United States Merchant Marine Academy. She could read nautical charts and plot a course. She even knew how to navigate using the stars.

We waited. And waited. And waited. I could not feel my toes anymore. Ma told me to stomp my feet. The prickly pain almost felt warm.

Slowly, the dot became a ship. Ma checked with her binoculars again.

"The pilothouse must be covered in ice—no telling what color it is from here," she said. Then a few minutes later she checked again and nearly whispered, "Ah, now I see the *C* on the stack!" The red *C* stood for Cleveland-Cliffs, the company that owned Papa's boat. I rubbed the iron ore in my pocket and sent out my heartbeat signals.

Buh-bump! Buh-bump! Buh-bump!

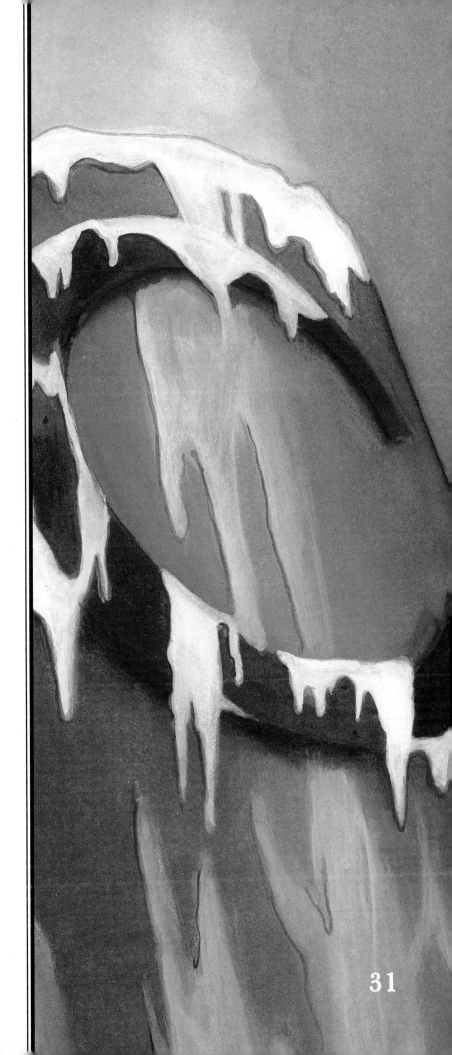

Far out from the canal, the ship fought against the choppy waves. Sometimes it seemed to stop moving. I knew that it could take a long, long time for the ship to reach us. I snuggled up against Ma's wool coat. She tucked the telltale lock of hair under her hat again and hugged me tightly. I closed my eyes and felt the taconite pellets.

I was dreaming about Ma knitting gazillions of red mittens, when I heard a commanding horn. One long blast, one short blast. One long blast, one short blast again. I kept my eyes shut and listened. A closer horn answered: one long blast, one short blast. Then one long blast, one short blast. It meant a ship wanted the bridge over the canal to lift up. Bells started clanging. Gates lowered to stop traffic. Slowly, the metal grid that spanned the cold water climbed up the lacy-steel bridge towers to let the ship pass beneath it.

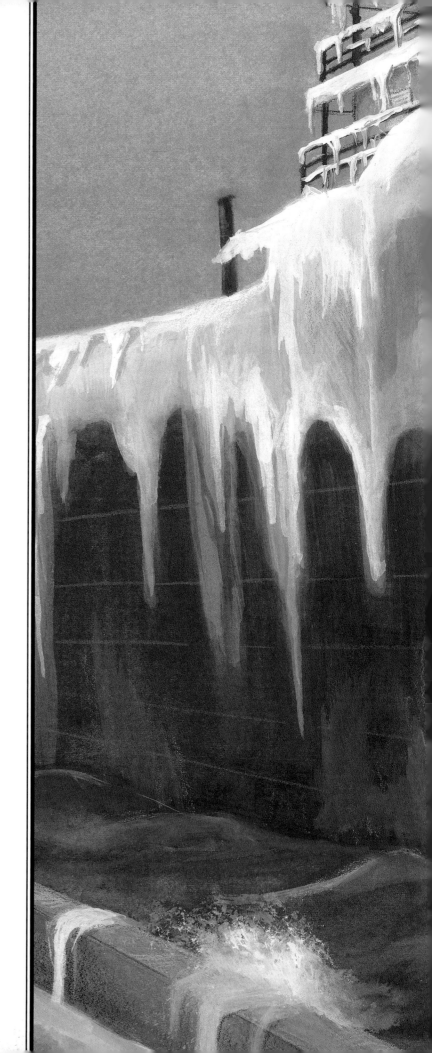

I waited to open my eyes. Minutes ticked away as the ship followed its course toward the harbor's safety. Many Cleveland-Cliffs ships sailed into Duluth this time of year. Maybe this ship was the *William G. Mather* or the *Cliffs Victory*. What if it wasn't Papa's boat? Would we sit in this bitterly cold wind all day? Could we?

Ma squeezed my shoulder gently again.

When I could not wait anymore, I opened my eyes and struggled to focus on the canal. Instead of crashing waves, I saw a floating tower of dark ice. I followed the iceberg upward, tilting my head so far back the scarf slid down to my chin.

Icicles as thick as a man's arm hung from the green pilothouse. I could barely read the ship's ice-drenched name—*Edward B. Greene*! Papa's ship was so close I could see the battened hatches under the frozen whitewash. I could even see the gold braids on Papa's fine uniform as he waved to me.

Suddenly, a horn blared one long blast, then two short blasts. All sailors knew that whistle code: **Greetings!**

"Toooooot! Toot! Toot!" I yelled back to my father. The three lucky pellets bounced in my pocket as I jumped up and waved. Ma jumped up, too, waving and laughing into the wind.

I decided to keep the pellets and my secret code, just in case Papa needed them again.

Taconite

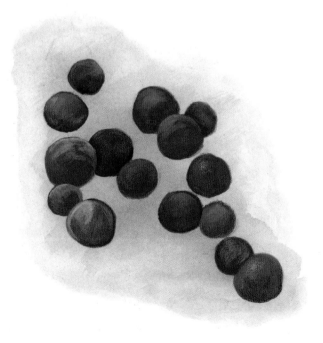

Taconite (TACK ah night) pellets come from dull gray or reddish taconite rock found mainly in Minnesota, Michigan, and parts of Canada. Huge machines grind the rock into powder and strong magnets pull out the iron. Mixers blend the powdered iron with clay and limestone to make small balls. Ovens bake and harden the pellets for easier shipping and faster processing in the steel mills. As in the past, trains and steamships haul the taconite from the northern mines to steelmakers near Lake Erie. Many vessels also carry taconite through the St. Lawrence Seaway to foreign ports.

The Great Lakes

The five Great Lakes stretch from Minnesota to New York and all but Lake Michigan touch both the United States and Canada. In 1959, the St. Lawrence Seaway opened a passage for deep-water vessels or "salties." The St. Lawrence Seaway includes all five freshwater lakes, the St. Lawrence River, and many rivers and canals that connect them. Shipping routes for iron ore, steel, petroleum, grain, and many other types of cargo now cover more than 2,000 miles between the Atlantic Ocean and the port of Duluth, Minnesota.

About the Author

Tracy Nelson Maurer grew up near the ports of Duluth, Minnesota and Superior, Wisconsin. Her grandfather, the late Captain Harvey C. Almstedt, skippered the steamship *Edward B. Greene* of the Cleveland-Cliffs' Great Lakes fleet. His sailing stories inspired this historically based book. Tracy has written many nonfiction children's books for schools and libraries. She lives near Minneapolis with her husband and two children. To learn more, visit www.TracyMaurerWriter.com.

Author Acknowledgments

Real-life sailors and their families inspired this work. The story features many authentic shipping references, and I'm grateful to Cleveland-Cliffs for granting permission to use its corporate insignias and steamship names. I extend my sincere appreciation to Wallace and Patricia Rohn; the *William G. Mather* Museum staff; Laura Jacobs, Lake Superior Maritime Collections, UW-S; Thom Holden, Director, Lake Superior Maritime Visitor Center; sailors and enthusiasts Wayne Bratton, Fred Sommer, Tom Massopust, Len Robinson and John Clark; Duluth photographers Kenneth Newham and Robin Bruelheide; the crew at Don Farleo Advertising & Design Company; and Alan Krysan and the exceptional team at Windward Publishing as well as Christina Rodriguez and Travis Wood. My deepest thanks goes to my mom, Lois Almstedt Nelson, and to my favorites: Mike, Meg, and Tommy.

About the Illustrator

Born overseas to multicultural parents, **Christina Rodriguez** grew up as an "Air Force brat," moving from place to place. She always loved to create art and earned her degree in Illustration from the Rhode Island School of Design. Christina works as a freelance illustrator and designer. She and her husband live with their dog in Stillwater, Minnesota. To learn more, visit www.ChristinaRodriguez.com.

Illustrator Acknowledgments

I would like to thank Tracy Nelson Maurer and her mother Lois Almstedt Nelson for lending me many books and family photos, as their heritage was the foremost inspiration in illustrating this book. I would also like to thank the fine folks at the *S.S. William A. Irvin* Ore Boat Museum for their patience and tolerance while I repeatedly wandered off the tour to take reference photos.

To learn more about shipping on the St. Lawrence Seaway, please visit www.stormcodes.com